Photography by Hugo Burnand

THE AUTHOR

Lisa Dennis is the wife of Ron, Team Principal of the McLaren Formula One team. She loves travelling the world, attending all the races. Her many amazing experiences – and her own inventive children – have inspired her to create Mac & Lauren.

PAUL RICARD
TEST CIRCUIT

FRANCE

Circuit Length:
2.640 miles (4.25km)

HOCKENHEIM
RACE CIRCUIT

GERMANY

Circuit Length:
4.239 miles (6.823km)

An imprint of Simon & Schuster UK Ltd. Africa House, 64-78 Kingsway, London WC2B 6AH
A Viacom Company
First published in Great Britain in 2002 by Simon & Schuster UK Ltd

A CIP catalogue record for this book is available from the British Library
ISBN 07434 50515
1 3 5 7 9 10 8 6 4 2

The sun shone high over the south of France as Mac and Lauren arrived at Paul Ricard, their favourite test track. Titan the transporter was with them, loaded up with a new, top-secret fuel that would make them go faster than ever in next week's German Grand Prix.

'I can't wait to get zooming round the track!' cried Mac.

'Hey, look,' said Lauren. 'Someone's got here before us!'

TITAN
MAC
1

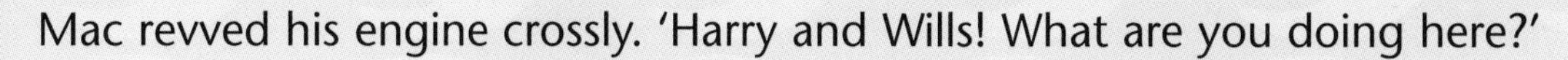

Mac revved his engine crossly. 'Harry and Wills! What are you doing here?'

'Not feeling too friendly, old boy?' teased Wills.

'We were meant to have the track all to ourselves!' Lauren explained.

'But it's fun to share, chaps!' said Harry.

'If you're so keen on sharing,' Mac answered wickedly…

REVS
10
HARRY
10
1

…'Share our dust!' Mac and Lauren soon forgot their worries as they raced faster and faster around the track.

Harry drove off to the pits in a bad mood. 'Mac and Lauren have never been so fast!' he muttered. 'I think I'll ask Titan what tyres they're using today.'

But Mac zoomed up behind him. 'So you came to spy on us, did you?' he said.

'Of course I didn't!' Harry said, and he roared away in a huff.

A few days later, Titan was thundering through the night on the long journey to Hockenheim, the race track in Germany. He was carrying Mac, Lauren, and barrels full of the new super-fuel.

'How about a break?' Titan yawned as he saw the signs for a rest stop.

'Good thinking,' Lauren called back. Titan pulled in and soon they had all fallen fast asleep.

P ½ km
ZZZZ

TAN
TITAN

Bruno and Mad Maddy were also on their way to Hockenheim. They were charging down the motorway in Brutus, their own transporter, when they spotted Titan fast asleep.

BRUTUS
4
4
4
OP
RET
OP
RET
OP
RET

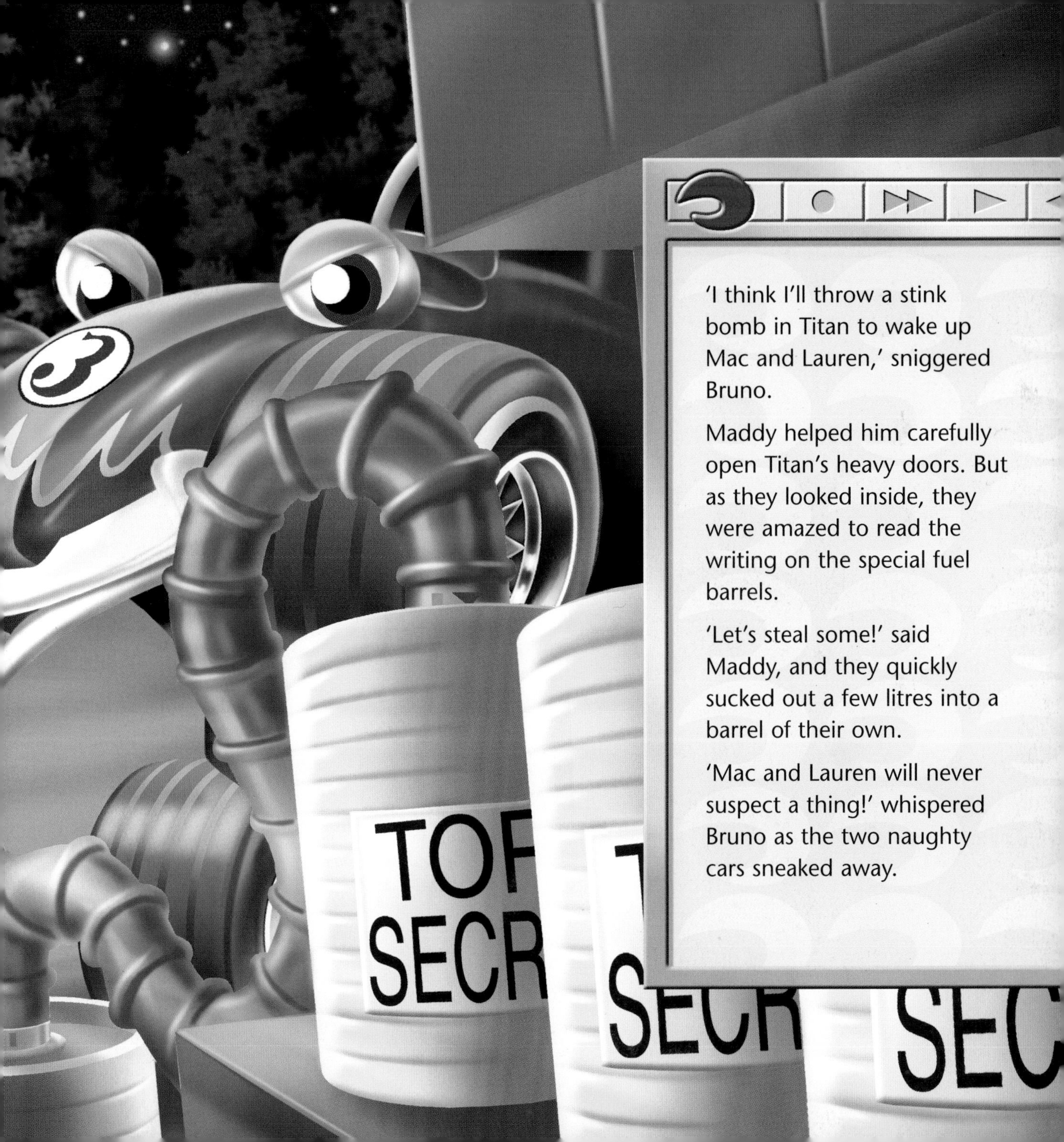

'I think I'll throw a stink bomb in Titan to wake up Mac and Lauren,' sniggered Bruno.

Maddy helped him carefully open Titan's heavy doors. But as they looked inside, they were amazed to read the writing on the special fuel barrels.

'Let's steal some!' said Maddy, and they quickly sucked out a few litres into a barrel of their own.

'Mac and Lauren will never suspect a thing!' whispered Bruno as the two naughty cars sneaked away.

On Saturday morning, before qualifying, Computer had a meeting with Mac and Lauren. 'When we filled Frankie Fueller, we were three litres short,' he boomed. 'Someone has stolen our secret fuel!'

'And I reckon we know who!' Mac roared, racing up to Harry. 'You were snooping on us in France – you must have stolen our special new fuel! Thief!'

Harry had never seen Mac so cross. 'I don't know what you're talking about, Mac!' he whined. 'Honest!'

Lauren spoke to Mac when he got back to the pits. 'Take it easy,' she told him. 'If Harry says he didn't do it, I believe him. He's our friend.'

'I know,' Mac sighed. 'But who else could've done it?'

Meanwhile, Bruno and Maddy had just enough of the secret fuel for qualifying.

'We were almost as fast as Mac and Lauren,' bragged Bruno.

'Yeah, and we'll be right behind them on the grid when the race starts,' gloated Maddy. 'But we still need to steal some more fuel if we want to win!'

SPEED

'I know,' said Bruno. 'Let's disguise our own Frankie Fueller to look like Mac and Lauren's. They'll fill him up with special fuel for us!'

But Wills overheard them as he drove by, and quickly slammed on his brakes. 'What bad sports!' he thought, and went off to tell Harry all about it. 'We must warn Mac and Lauren!'

'But Mac called me a thief!' moaned Harry.

'Two wrongs don't make a right,' Wills reminded him.

Mac listened to Wills's story and sighed. 'I know Bruno and Maddy are always up to no good,' he said. 'But you'd stand up for Harry no matter what!'

'Not if he was lying I wouldn't,' said Wills sniffily. 'Just watch out when you're filling your fuellers. One of those Frankies will be Bruno's in disguise!'

'There's an easy way to learn who the real thieves are,' said Lauren. 'Let's mix up some **special** fuel! If Titan spots any dodgy fuellers about…'

'…he can let them have it!' Mac laughed. 'Let's get busy!'

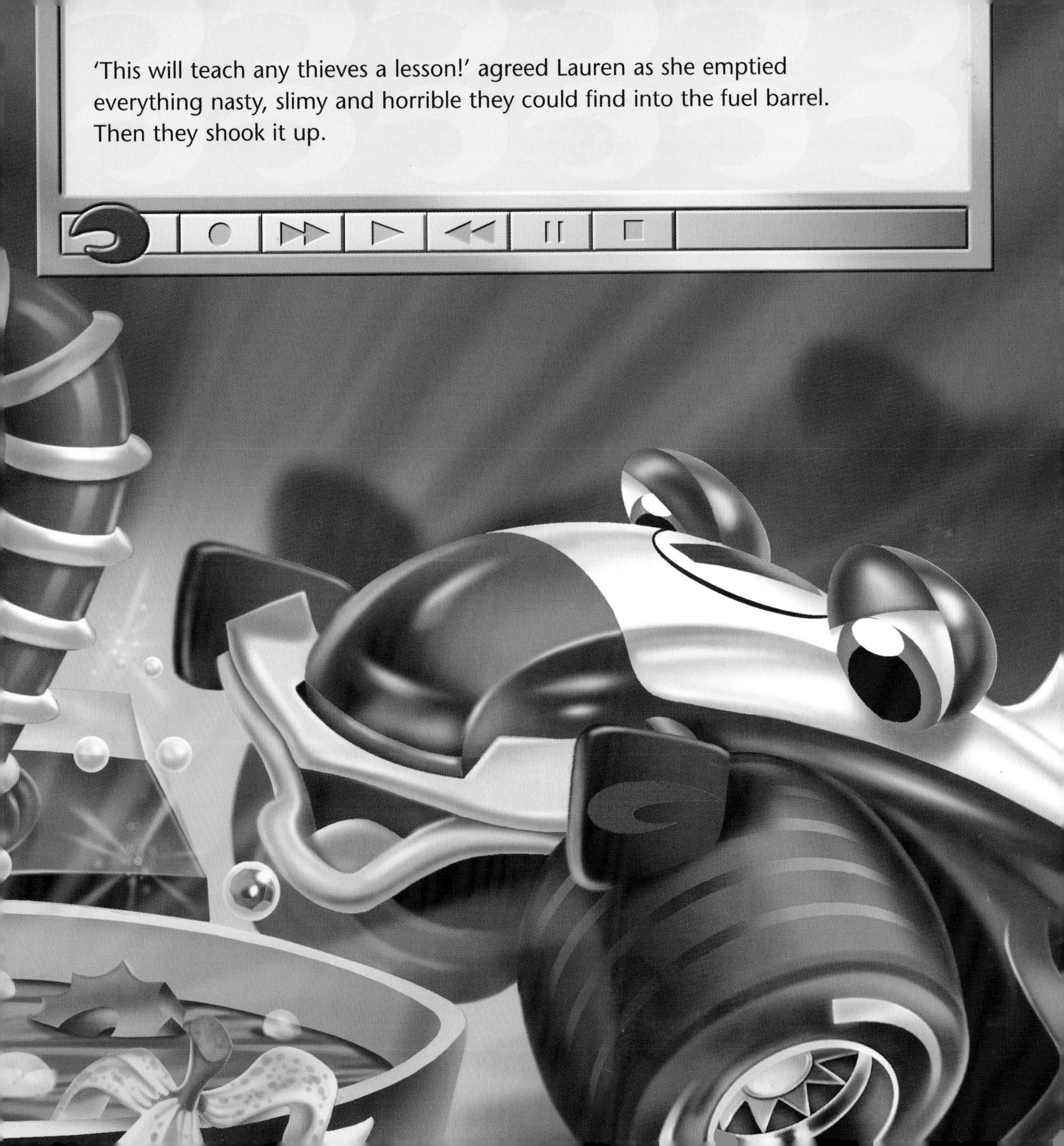

'This will teach any thieves a lesson!' agreed Lauren as she emptied everything nasty, slimy and horrible they could find into the fuel barrel. Then they shook it up.

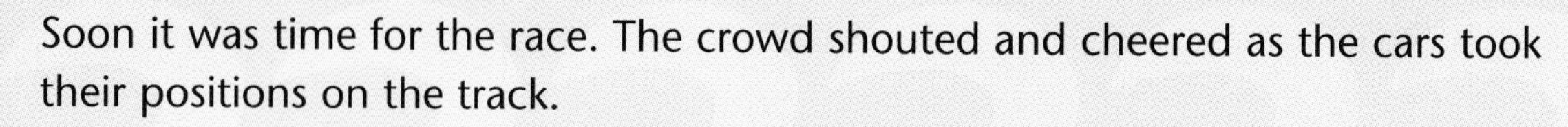

Soon it was time for the race. The crowd shouted and cheered as the cars took their positions on the track.

'1,2,3,4,5,' counted Mac to himself as the lights lit up overhead on the gantry.

'Lights out! GO!' revved Lauren. 'I can't wait until the first pit stop,' she giggled over her radio to Computer. 'We'll see then who the culprits are!'

LAUREN
LAUREN
MAC
MAC
GO!

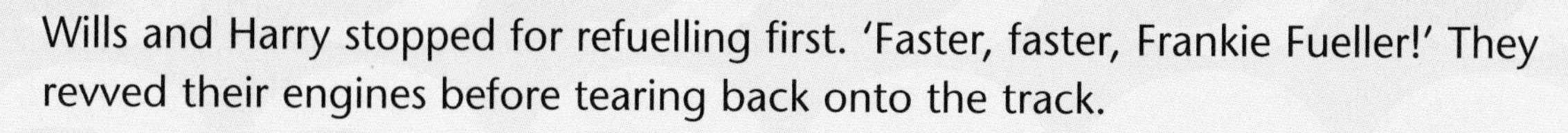

Wills and Harry stopped for refuelling first. 'Faster, faster, Frankie Fueller!' They revved their engines before tearing back onto the track.

Roxy and Lucky came in next, and Mac and Lauren soon followed. 'Now the fun starts,' Mac roared back from the pit lane.

'Mac and Lauren's super-fuel will soon have us taking the lead!' sniggered Bruno as he and Maddy skidded to a halt for refuelling.

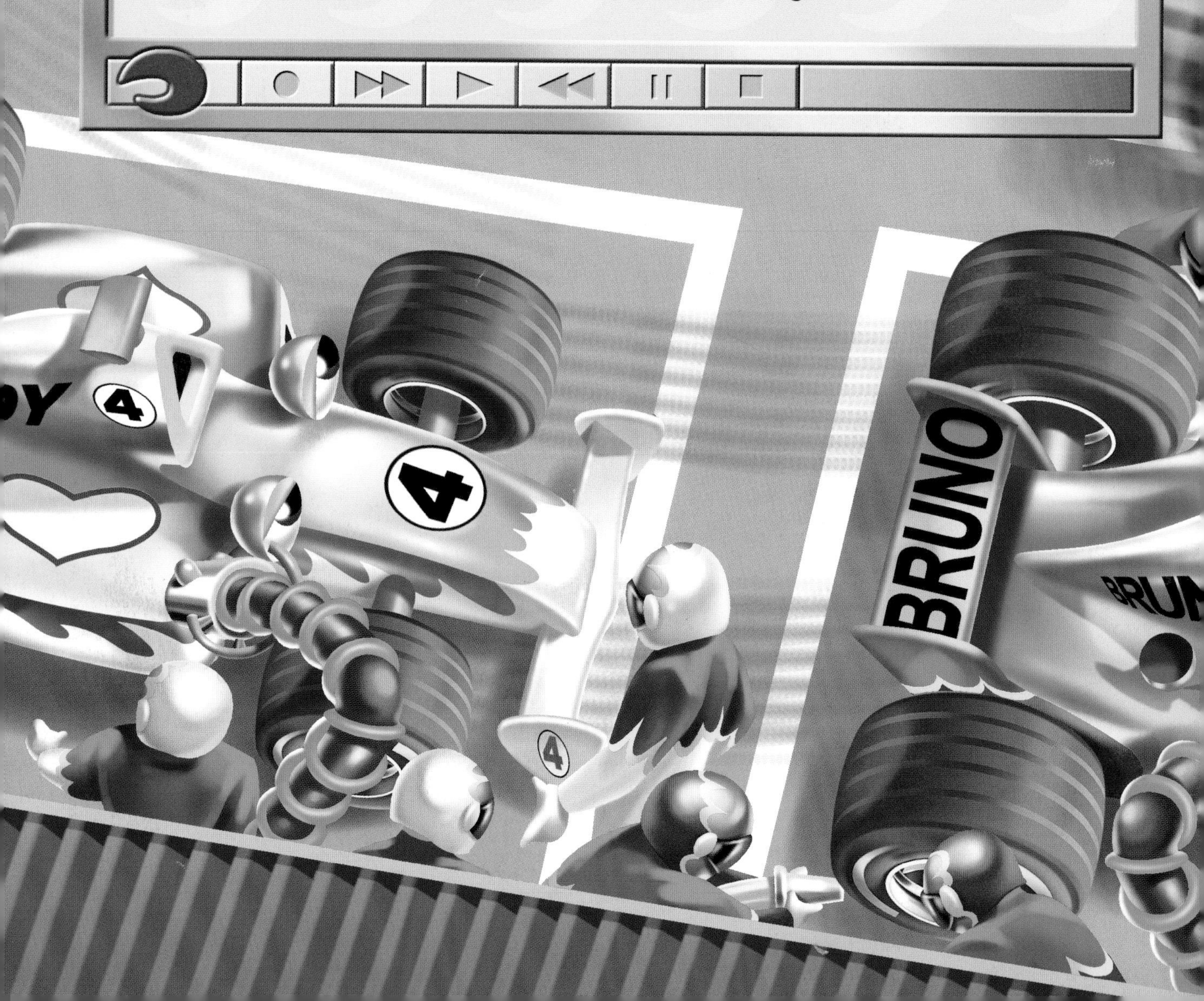

1
MAC
1
SLØW!
3
3

But by the time they'd finished the next lap they knew something was wrong.

'Look at my paintwork!' shrieked Maddy as she came out in spots.

'Bulging bumps!' cried Bruno as his chassis started to swell and bubble.

SNIFF!
BRUNO
BRUNO

Before they'd completed two more laps, Maddy and Bruno exploded into clouds of thick black smoke! They skidded in puddles of their own smelly fuel until they rattled to a halt. The crowds jeered and laughed at them.

'Not fair!' whined Maddy.

'We've been tricked!' Bruno moaned.

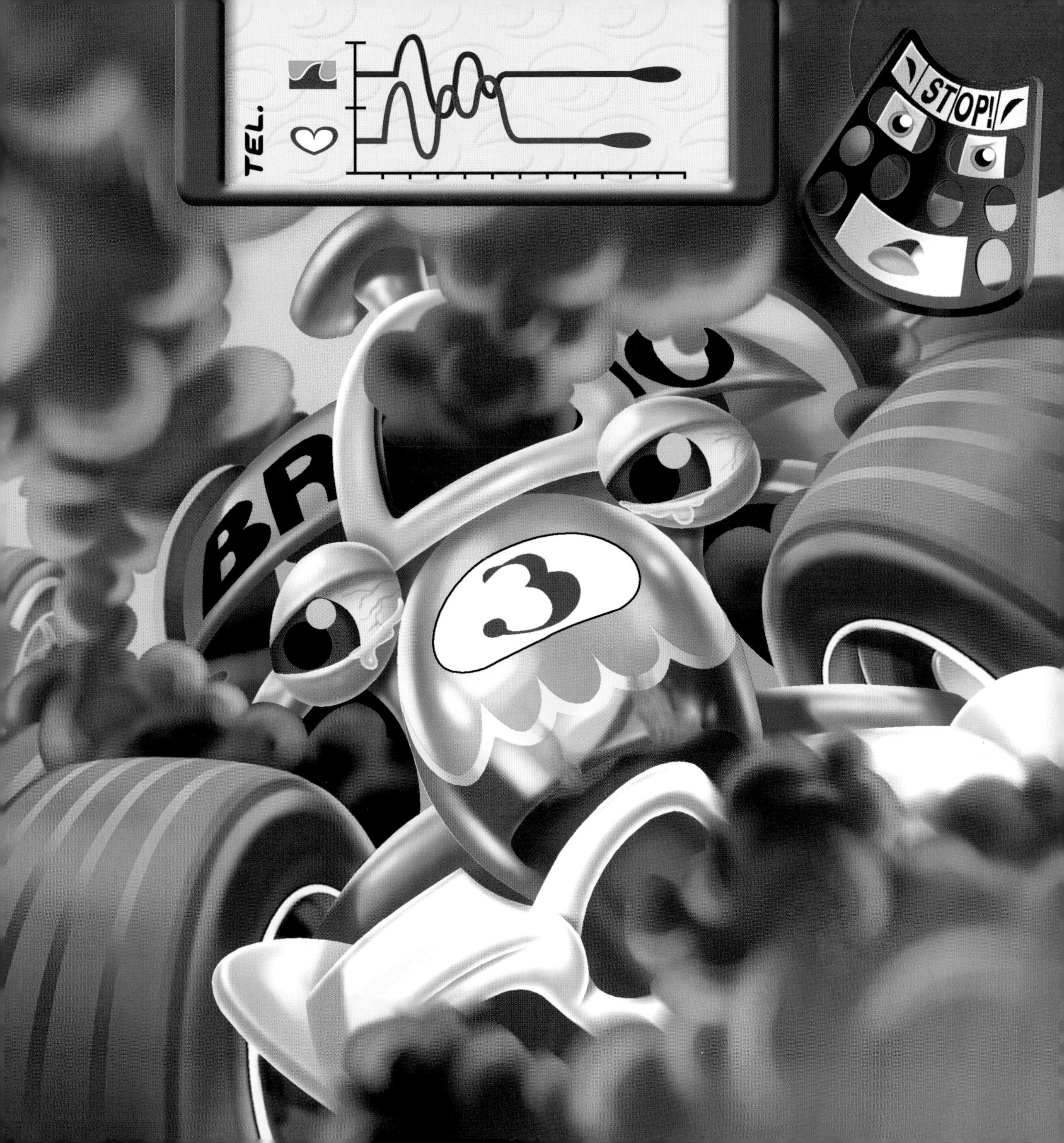
TEL.
STOP!
3

FLAG
1
MAC
10
HARRY
4

'Bouncing bungees, you two are slippery and smelly,' choked Christian Crane as he struggled to clear the track.

'I was wrong to blame Harry,' thought Mac. As he rounded the bend he saw Harry was stuck in the gooey fuel. 'But now I'll make it up to him!'

Mac dragged Harry free and towed him along!

Lauren zoomed across the finish line in first place. Mac came in second. Harry took third place and Wills flew past in fourth. The fans went wild!

'That was another great race!' hummed Lauren happily. 'And I can't wait for the next one!'

'Neither can I!' Mac agreed, and smiled at Wills and Harry. 'Especially now we're all friends again!'

RACE INFORMATION

CAR GRAPHICS

 MAC

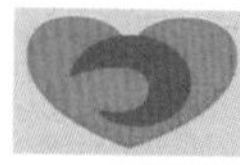 LAUREN

 ROXY

 LUCKY

 WILLS

 HARRY

 MARCO

 FRANCO

 MADDY

 BRUNO

INFORMATION SCREENS

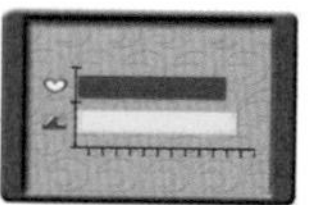

SPEED
– shows lap times

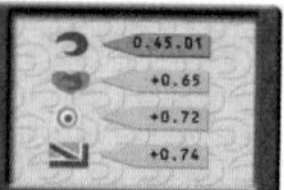

RACE POSITION
– shows leader

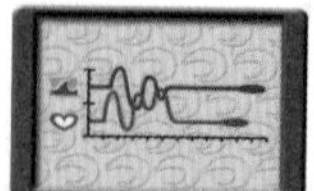

TELEMETRY
– shows technical info

TEMPERATURE
– temperature read-out

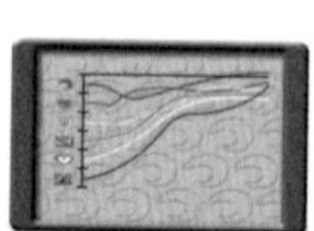

REVS
– shows engine rpm

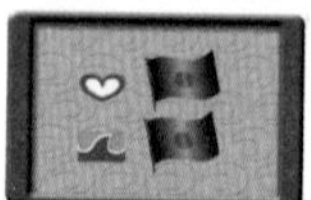

FLAG
– shows current situation

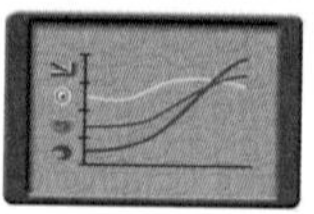

ACCELERATION
– shows acceleration